# Where Will They Go?

by Elias Edwards
illustrated by Mary Peterson

## Harcourt
SCHOOL PUBLISHERS

Printed in China

ISBN-13: 978-0-15-358411-4
ISBN-10: 0-15-358411-4

Ordering Options
ISBN 10: 0-15-358356-8 (Grade K On-Level Collection)
ISBN 13: 978-0-15-358356-8 (Grade K On-Level Collection)
ISBN 10: 0-15-360663-0 (package of 5)
ISBN 13: 978-0-15-360663-2 (package of 5)

4 5 6 7 8 9 10   0940   15 14 13 12 11 10 09

They are in a cab.

Where will they go?

Look where the cab will go.

They are in a jet.

Where will they go?

They will get in a van.

They are in the van.
Where will they go?

Look at where they go.

They are here!
They will have jam.